RACE THE WILD

GREAT REEF GAMES

RACE THE WILD

ARE YOU READY TO RUN THE WILDEST RACE OF YOUR LIFE?

Course #1: Rain Forest Relay

Course #2: Great Reef Games

RACE THE WILD

GREAT REEF GAMES

·BY **KRISTIN EARHART**·
·ILLUSTRATED BY **EDA KABAN**·

SCHOLASTIC INC.

TO BARBARA, WHO iS MY FAVORiTE SUPER SMARTiE —KJE

Text copyright © 2015 by Kristin Earhart
Illustrations copyright © 2015 by Scholastic Inc.

All rights reserved. Published by Scholastic Inc., *Publishers since 1920*. SCHOLASTIC and associated logos are trademarks and/or registered trademarks of Scholastic Inc.

The publisher does not have any control over and does not assume any responsibility for author or third-party websites or their content.

No part of this publication may be reproduced, stored in a retrieval system, or transmitted in any form or by any means, electronic, mechanical, photocopying, recording, or otherwise, without written permission of the publisher. For information regarding permission, write to Scholastic Inc., Attention: Permissions Department, 557 Broadway, New York, NY 10012.

This book is a work of fiction. Names, characters, places, and incidents are either the product of the author's imagination or are used fictitiously, and any resemblance to actual persons, living or dead, business establishments, events, or locales is entirely coincidental.

ISBN 978-0-545-77354-6

12 11 10 9 8 7 6 5 4 3 2   15 16 17 18 19 20/0

Printed in the U.S.A.   40
First printing 2015

Book design by Yaffa Jaskoll

CHAPTER 1

GREAT REEF, GREAT RACE

Sage Stevens surveyed the beach bungalow and took a deep breath. The smell of the salt in the air reminded her why she was there. It wasn't for the lunch buffet that stretched the length of the banquet room. Nor was it to make friends with the other contestants. She didn't even care about the breathtaking ocean views and sending home postcards with pictures of tropical fish.

The only reason Sage was in Australia was to win the next leg of *The Wild Life*, a competition where kids traveled the world and explored the wonders of the animal kingdom.

Sage twisted one earring to keep calm. She'd been up since dawn. Despite the time change, she hadn't needed an alarm clock. Her brain was wired for competition. She had gone ahead and woken up her three teammates using the cuckoo call that they'd picked up on the first part of the race. The birdcall had come in handy in the Amazon rain forest, but no one had been happy to hear the chirping cackle again at 6:47 that morning. If Sage had known the second stage of the race wouldn't start until after lunch, she might have let her teammates sleep. After all, they'd need their energy for the challenges ahead.

Sage nudged Mari so they didn't lose their place in line. Mari was only a year younger, but Sage still felt the need to look out for her. Maybe it was because Mari reminded Sage of her sister. They were both Smarties, for one. "Smartie" was a name Sage used for kids who were unusually intelligent, so smart they couldn't hide it. Mari could spout facts about nature in her sleep. Her knowledge about animals and habitats had made all the difference to Team Red on the first leg of the race.

"Good luck holding on to first place."

It took Sage a moment to register that the comment was aimed at her.

She glanced over her shoulder. "Thanks," she responded, matching stares with Eliza, the tallest member of Team Purple. Eliza was a Smartie, too, and she wanted everyone to know it.

"I heard this part of the race is about power. Brainpower." Eliza had a smug smile. Her lips stretched out in a flat line and didn't let her teeth show.

"Team Red is up for it," Sage answered. She reached past the other girl for a biscuit. "Excuse me," she said, and turned away.

As they made their way through the buffet line, Sage put two links of sausage onto Mari's empty plate. "You have to eat if you're going to compete," she said absentmindedly. It was the phrase her track coaches always used when they were handing out snack bars before a big meet.

Mari looked up at Sage with her deep brown eyes. "I'm a vegetarian," she said, her words soft but even. "I don't eat meat."

"In that case, I'll take those," Sage said, piercing the sausages with a fork. "There are all kinds of pasta and cheese and peanut butter sandwiches at that end," she suggested, motioning to the far side of the room. The long table was crowded with every kind of food imaginable: fruit, grilled fish, nuts, jerky, veggies, and dips.

Mari nodded, her thick dark braid swaying as she walked away.

As soon as her plate was full, Sage looked for the other two members of their team. She spotted their bright red T-shirts, and headed toward the table they'd claimed. Russell's plate was piled high with deli-style sandwiches and fruit. Dev's plate, on the other hand, looked like the picture on a poster for the five essential food groups. There were equal portions of each protein and vegetable. Sage noted that his peas did not touch his carrots or mashed potatoes. She had seen inside Dev's hiking backpack—it was just as organized.

Just as Mari and Sage sat down across from their teammates, Dev and Russell stopped talking. Russell hadn't said a thing to Sage since she'd woken him up that morning, but he had shot her a few foul glances. She wondered if they didn't want her to hear what they were saying. It was a moment before she realized that a hush had fallen over the entire bungalow.

That's when Bull Gordon strode into the room, the heels of his cowboy boots announcing his entrance. *The Wild Life* race's host wore his trademark fedora, an enormous shark tooth tucked into the leather band. Like all great adventurers, he had a notable scar on his tanned chin. He also had disarmingly white teeth, which he flashed at all the contestants as he approached the front of the room.

"So you survived the Amazon," Bull announced, one thumb hooked through the belt loop of his jeans. "All the teams logged impressive times, but some fared better than others with the actual clues."

When they heard this, the members of Team Red locked gazes. The clues had been their strength. They had stolen the win from Team Green in the last moments of the first leg, all because Russell had known the answer to the final question.

"But that's in the past," Bull continued. "The Great Barrier Reef has its own set of challenges. It is one of the most diverse marine habitats in the world: a string of living coral so long it can be

seen from space." As he scanned the room, his eyes narrowed. "It's also fragile. Life here is a delicate balance, and you have to respect it. If you don't follow the guidelines, you will get a time penalty . . . or worse."

Sage's forehead crinkled as she tried to figure out what Bull was saying. Would they get disqualified? There was no way her team was going to be disqualified. She would not let that happen.

"So, protect the reef first," Bull announced. "Then protect yourselves. You are in Australia, where everything is bigger, more beautiful, and more dangerous. You have to get serious."

Sage smiled tightly. Bull Gordon could save his advice for the other contestants. They all seemed like amateurs. Sage was born serious, and she planned to win.

EXTREMELY SMALL, EXTREMELY IMPORTANT

While coral reefs cover less than two percent of the ocean floor, they provide shelter for one-quarter of the ocean's animals.

The Great Barrier Reef is the largest group of reefs in the world. Together, these reefs stretch nearly 1,500 miles along the northeastern coast of Australia.

The reef is home to more than 1,500 species of fish. The fish dine on everything from the sea grass that grows in the shallow waters to tiny plants and animals that float in from the ocean.

When they aren't eating, they are hiding! The reef, with its many nooks and crannies, is a good place for that.

The fish are hiding from predators. More than 130 species of sharks and rays call the reef home. From the bottom-feeding nurse shark to the large tiger shark—a super predator—many hunters depend on the reef for food.

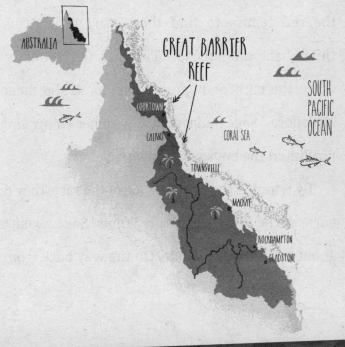

AUSTRALIA

GREAT BARRIER REEF

SOUTH PACIFIC OCEAN

COOKTOWN

CAIRNS

CORAL SEA

TOWNSVILLE

MACKAY

ROCKHAMPTON

GLADSTONE

CHAPTER 2

A TREASURE MAP

Without a word, Bull Gordon handed each team an envelope and exited the room. Sage tore open the red team's to find their start time. "One thirty," she announced. "That's in five minutes. Go to the bathroom, grab travel food, and meet back here." Sage nudged Mari with her elbow and prompted the boys with a hasty glance.

By winning the previous leg of the race, they'd earned the first departure time. Sage wasn't about to let it go to waste. On the way back from the bathroom, she grabbed an energy bar—then several more, just in case her teammates needed them.

It still wasn't clear how they had all ended up together: Dev, Russell, Mari, and Sage. It seemed like a lot of the kids on the other teams had known one another before the race. Russell had a bunch of friends on Team Green, but the organizers had put him on Team Red. Sage thought that was kind of weird. The organizers seemed to like to group certain kinds of kids together. Team Purple, Eliza's crew, was full of Smarties. The blue team members were all über-athletes. But Team Red didn't fit that mold. They didn't have much in common with one another.

Sage, Mari, and Dev had all sent in single applications. Then the organizers had plucked Russell from his friends and matched them together: four complete strangers. Sage didn't like leaving things to luck. She wasn't sure about working with three people she didn't know. But so far, they had made a pretty good team. They each had a role that helped the team win. While they all knew about wildlife, Mari's knowledge was deeper and her brain faster with the clues. Dev was a tech guru with a mechanical mind. Russell was their strength, not only in body, but also in spirit. And Sage was the leader. It was her job to keep them working like a team.

One of the race agents was at the door with a clipboard. Sage stood next to her and watched for the others, her mind churning, trying to anticipate the challenges the day would bring. When the whole team was there, the agent glanced up, her thumb hovering above the knob on a stop-watch. "The next team starts in ten minutes," she said. "Make the most of it." Sage nodded. As soon as the agent's thumb moved, Sage yelled, "Go, go, go!" Her muscles exploded, all the tension from waiting turned into energy. At last, the race had started and they were on the move. Sage felt more at ease now. She glanced back. Her teammates were all behind her. The bright sun glinted off the white sand and clear blue water, a row of palm trees offering the only shade.

Sage would race anywhere. It didn't really matter that this was paradise. The sand felt hot on her feet, filling the creases of her water sandals.

Even though it was winter in Australia, the sun's rays were still strong. As Sage neared

the dock at the far end of the beach, she saw Bull Gordon. He was standing with Javier, Team Red's guide.

"We're coming!" Sage called, waving as she came to a stop. She was certain her teammates were all relieved to see Javier. He had been a good chaperone in the Amazon.

"Team Red," Bull began, "you are currently in first place. Therefore, you get first choice of the yachts. The yacht will be your home base until you reach the end of the race course tomorrow."

Sage's eyes swept over the multilevel vessels. "We'll take the one at the far end of the dock. The *Aqua Adventure*."

Bull Gordon looked to the other team members.

"It looks like they all have about the same type of motor, so I don't think any one vessel has more power," Dev commented. Sage recalled how the green team had managed to get a much faster boat during the last leg.

"In that case, it doesn't matter to me," Russell said with a shrug. Mari nodded.

"Very well, *Aqua Adventure* is yours. Remember to respect the reef," Bull said with a stern gaze. "Javier, give them this clue on board."

Javier took a red folder from Bull and nodded. Bull glanced at the four contestants. "What are you waiting for?" he asked. "It's a race!"

With that, they were off.

Sage was the first to the yacht. She waited for Javier on deck to make sure she'd get ahold of the clue. The rest of the team gathered around as she opened the folder. "Treasure map," she read aloud.

"Awesome," Russell said. "Do you think there's a real treasure, like with jewels?"

"Let me read the clue and we'll find out." Sage tried not to sound huffy. "This is a map. It will show you how to keep the ocean's greatest treasure safe. Find the right path to the coordinates and you will find your next challenge."

"That isn't hard," Dev said, gesturing to the clue. "It's just using north, south, east, and west and finding the coordinates on the map. We locate the spot and go."

"No," Sage contended. "Check it out. This map is like a puzzle. It's all different colors."

"It's a zoning map," Russell figured out. "Look. It tells you where you can go and what you can do. There's no fishing here, and you can't even swim in the places that are pink."

They all stared at the numbers on the clue and the map for a while. "All right, team," Sage announced, tracing around the coast of Australia with her finger. "We need a path that will take us out beyond these parts of the reef, and we can't go through restricted spots."

At once, Russell, Dev, and Mari settled at the small table in the boat's seating area and got to work finding the best route.

"The clue said this was a treasure map. So, in this scenario," Dev thought out loud, "the ocean's greatest treasure is—"

"The reef, of course," Mari finished for him. "The map shows us how to keep the reef safe."

It wasn't long before they had highlighted the

fastest—and safest—path for a boat of their size to take. Sage ran along the yacht's galley and handed the proposed route to the captain. The man in the white hat with a golden anchor above the brim looked at the sheet and nodded.

Sage smiled when she heard the engines fire up. She looked at her watch. Her team was fast. She dared the other teams to try to catch them.

CREATURE FEATURE

CORAL

SCIENTIFIC NAME: many families, including Acroporidae and Faviidae

TYPE: Anthozoa, along with sea anemones and sea fans

RANGE: in shallow, tropical waters

FOOD: small plants and animals called plankton; sometimes tiny fish

The coral that makes up the reef is an animal. Actually, it is hundreds—even thousands—of tiny animals living together in a colony. A single coral creature is called a polyp.

Most kinds of coral build their own skeleton. They do this by releasing small amounts of limestone each day. The type of coral determines what shape the skeleton will take: staghorn coral looks like antlers, brain coral looks like a brain, and lettuce coral looks like the makings of a healthy salad.

Like any living creature, coral needs certain things to survive. Coral needs food. It needs a healthy, safe place to grow. The seawater cannot be too hot or cold. It can't be too dirty. All these things contribute to the health of the reef.

CHAPTER 3

SAILING IN THE SKY

The trip was choppy. The yacht pitched against the waves for almost an hour. Sage couldn't sit still, so she went up to the deck where she was spritzed by the sea's spray. When the boat chugged to a stop, Sage searched the horizon. She spotted a small, lush island with a ring of sand all around, but it was too far away to swim.

She stormed down the ship's stairs to find Javier sitting with the rest of the team. "What's up?" she demanded. "We're here, right? Did we get another clue?"

"Give it a minute, and you'll figure out what to do," Javier answered. "Why don't you put on a wet suit while you wait? It'll keep you from getting too cold, and it will protect you from box jellyfish."

"Jellyfish?" Russell repeated, his body straightening with a jerk. "Those things are super venomous. No way am I going in that water if there are jellyfish."

"You're right," Javier agreed without sounding concerned. "Some species are extremely toxic. One touch of a tentacle can kill you, but they aren't common in winter months. We'll all be on the lookout, and the suit is good protection. If you see one, everyone has to get out, pronto."

The other three were busy forcing their limbs into the thick fabric of the wet suits, but Russell was full of doubt.

"Don't worry, man," Dev tried to reassure his teammate. "If you get stung, we can just pee on you." He tried to keep a straight face. "I read that pee can neutralize the toxins."

"That's an old wives' tale," Mari said as she pulled her braid from the back of her suit. "White vinegar is what doctors used to recommend, but even that might make the tentacles release more venom. The treatment is complicated, so it's best just to avoid getting stung altogether."

"Exactly," Russell said, his face expressionless. "And not just because I don't want Dev to pee on me."

Sage was just as relieved as Russell that Mari had dispelled that rumor.

"If you're worried, check the water for tiny animals like shrimp," Mari suggested. "You probably aren't going to find any jellyfish if they can't find any food."

Sage watched as Russell scanned the waves around the boat. It was obvious how much he trusted Mari's advice, because he heaved a sigh of relief. The water looked clear.

Just then, a motorboat appeared from behind the nearby island. Javier waved it down. "Get ready for your first challenge," he announced. He held out a canvas box and raised the lid. Inside was what looked like a smartphone, with a short antenna. "The ancam!" Dev declared, plunging his hand into the box.

"You sound so excited," Russell said in a mocking tone. Dev had hated the ancam at first, but had quickly mastered the tiny device that combined a walkie-talkie and camera. It was how they received directions and clues from the race organizers. It was also how they submitted their answers, so they could move on to the next clue.

"It's time," said Javier. "Get yourselves over to that boat."

"You got it?" Sage asked Dev, making sure he would take charge of their communications device. Dev held up the ancam and gave a confident grin.

Sage instinctively checked for both earrings, then dove in. The chill of the water made everything feel real. The race really was on now. With powerful strokes, she made her way to the other vessel.

After she climbed the ladder to the small deck, she looked back at her teammates. Dev wasn't far behind. His thick black hair was even straighter than usual, wet against his dark skin. Russell, despite his athletic frame and busy schedule of team sports, did not appear to be a strong swimmer. His kick was sloppy, and his breathing lacked an even rhythm. But Mari was struggling even more. When she finally reached the ladder, Sage reached out and gave her a hand. Mari looked disoriented with the salt water streaming down her tanned face. "You okay?" Sage asked.

"I think so," Mari answered, immediately sitting on the bench at the side of the deck.

Sage turned to the boat's captain and her first mate. Both wore long-sleeved rash guards for sun protection. With the same sparkly blue eyes and space between their front teeth, they looked like mother and son.

"Hi," Sage said. "We're part of *The Wild Life*."

"We know," answered the woman. "That's why we're here. I'm Gayle. This is Cole."

"We've got our next clue!" Dev announced, holding up the ancam. "I'll read it."

Two will start by flying high
To get a prime view from the sky.
Search and it will be no fluke
When your team sights a true fluke.

"Yuck. They need to get new writers," Dev declared. "You can't rhyme a word with the same word."

"But they have different meanings," Mari insisted.

"It doesn't matter. It's horrendous. And embarrassing."

"Who cares?" Sage called out, throwing up her arms. "We have a clue!" She turned back to Gayle. "Is this a parasail boat?" she asked, eyeing the gear near the boat's stern.

"Sure is. I need two volunteers."

"Dev, you should come with me," Sage said as she grabbed a pair of binoculars. When he paused, she added, "You're the one with the ancam."

Dev looked to Mari and Russell, then stepped into place next to Sage. There was a blur of buckles and snaps and straps as they put on life jackets and harnesses.

"Mari, any advice?" Sage asked.

"Well," Mari began, "there are fish called flukes, but I don't think any live around here, or are big enough to see from way up there." Mari squinted as she looked into the sky. "So you must be looking for a whale fluke—two flukes make up a whale's tail. You can see them when humpback whales breach. That's when they throw themselves out of the water. It's really beautiful."

Sage nodded. Maybe she should have chosen Mari to parasail with her. But Dev was the techie. She knew he'd get the best shot.

"Now is a good time to see humpbacks," Mari continued. "They've just migrated. Even in winter, the Great Barrier Reef is warmer than the Antarctic."

With breakneck speed, Gayle and Cole latched Sage into place on the small gondola. It reminded Sage of a ski lift. Dev paused, several steps away. His eyes seemed to be darting around, focusing on one thing and then another. At last, he came forward so Gayle and Cole could strap him in, too.

With the pull of a lever, Gayle released the parachute, which billowed behind the boat. The sail lifted and took Sage and Dev with it. Sage felt her stomach lurch.

"What were you looking at back there?" she asked.

"I was trying to figure out if this thing was

safe," Dev yelled over the swirling wind. "My dad would freak out if he could see me."

"Why?"

"He's an engineer. He is very concerned with the way things work."

Sage had been so set on the race that she hadn't even paused to think about safety. With all that had happened in the last year, she was surprised she hadn't considered it. But her focus was always on the finish line. "Remember, we're looking for whales," she said, concentrating on things she could control. "Breaching whales, so that we can see a fluke."

Sage took in the full view. They were now hundreds of feet in the air. Below them, the water was deep blue. Toward the mainland, she could see the reef. The water there was shallow and appeared much brighter. She could see how it was many reefs, hugging the coast. They looked like turquoise jewels from up high, strung together like an expensive necklace. It was hard to believe that something so big was alive—and that the animals that made the reef were so tiny.

"It's amazing up here," Sage yelled. The wind plastered loose strands of sun-bleached hair across her face.

"Yeah," Dev agreed. "I wish Russell and Mari could see it."

"Yeah," she said.

"Check it out!" Dev demanded, pointing at the ancam. "They added a telephoto lens! They kind of had to. We could never get a decent whale shot without it." Mari had told them that she had read in the folder about how there was a buffer zone for whale watching. No boat could get within a hundred yards of a whale for safety reasons.

Dev lifted the handheld device to his eye and tried to focus in on something below. "Hey, look," he said excitedly.

"What?" Sage asked hopefully.

"Russell's driving the boat."

"I thought you were worried about safety," Sage said.

"They won't let him do anything drastic," Dev answered, but just as he said it, the gondola took a dip.

"Whoa!" Sage yelled. It felt like all her organs had jumped into her throat. "What was that?"

Dev scanned the water's surface. "They must have spotted something."

Sage peered through her binoculars. "It's too bright. I can't see anything."

Dev leaned forward, ancam at the ready. "That's probably why they slowed down, so we would drop and get a better view."

Really? Sage thought Russell was just messing with them, wasting time.

They dipped again, and Sage saw a white-spotted whale tail disappear under the sapphire-blue water. "There!" Sage yelled. Almost immediately, a smaller whale torpedoed out of the water.

The young whale raised its fin in the air. Then it landed sideways with a bubbly white splash. The last thing to disappear was the tail, marked with white splotches and a ruffled trim. Dev's fingers worked quickly. *Click, click, click.*

"Did you get it?"

Dev held out the ancam, and they looked at the shots.

"They're kind of blurry," Sage said with concern. "But that one's the best."

"Cross your fingers," Dev murmured, and punched SEND.

The parasail had been descending at a steady rate, and Russell was still driving the boat.

"We're about to hit the water," said Sage.

"He'll pull up," Dev said, unconcerned.

He'd better, Sage thought, because this wasn't some joyride. They needed to be in position to take another picture, in case the first one wasn't approved.

Sage shivered as her toes dragged in the chilly water, and then the boat sped up. Within seconds, the wind had lifted the parachute and gondola a hundred feet.

"It was approved!" Dev called out.

"Phew!" Sage cried, and gave the signal for Cole to reel them in. She could wait until they were safe on board the boat—and reunited with Russell and Mari—to hear the next clue.

CREATURE FEATURE

HUMPBACK WHALES

SCIENTIFIC NAME: *Megaptera*

novaeangliae

TYPE: mammal

RANGE: Arctic, Atlantic, and Pacific Oceans

FOOD: plankton, small crustaceans, and fish

Humpback whales are not fish. They don't have gills. Like other mammals, they have lungs. A humpback breathes through two blowholes on top of its head and can stay underwater for up to twenty minutes.

Humpbacks migrate every year from frigid waters near the poles to more tropical waters, where they feed on plankton, krill, and small fish. As a type of baleen whale, they do not have teeth, but have baleen plates, which are like giant toothbrush-style filters that trap small food in the whale's mighty mouth.

While humpbacks have deep blue bodies, their fins are often partially white. Their tails can be marked with white as well. These special markings and the notches at the end of the tail are unique to each whale, like a human's fingerprint. Scientists use these details to keep track of whales in the wild.

CHAPTER 4

CLUED IN

"**W**e could barely see the whale," Mari said. Sage could tell she was disappointed. If the race organizers had not accepted Dev's picture, Team Red would have had to try to get a closer shot.

"I really love those big guys," Mari mumbled, more to herself than anyone else. Sage actually had a soft spot for whales, too. Ever since her first-grade teacher, Ms. Sarah, had taught her class about blubber by doing a cool science experiment, she'd found them fascinating. Ms. Sarah had used the same fluffy-looking white baking ingredient that Sage's mom used for making piecrusts. The experiment had shown how blubber helps keep whales and other large marine animals warm in near-freezing water. It was awesome.

"We need to keep moving," Sage said, half wishing they could stick around so Mari could get a better view. "Look at all the other parasails. We can't be the only team that got the picture on the first try."

"Sage is right," Dev confirmed. "And now we've got the next clue." He read it out loud.

Reef animals must compete
For space and for the food they eat.
So the smart ones plot and scheme

And work together as a team.

Find and submit three examples.

"So we're looking for examples of symbiosis, right?" Dev said.

"My science teacher called it *mutualism*," Sage offered. "But I think it's the same idea. Two different organisms living together and depending on each other."

"And both get something out of it," Russell added.

Sage glanced at Mari. The other girl gave a slight nod and looked back at the ocean. It was weird that Mari hadn't commented on the clue yet. Normally she would have rattled off a dozen answers by now.

Javier gave them a choice. They could look for examples while swimming around the reef, or they could all get in a glass-bottomed boat and view the reef from there.

"How are we going to communicate in the water? Do we get underwater two-way radios?" Dev asked, rubbing his hands together in hopeful anticipation.

"Nice try," Javier said. "But if you want to talk it through, the boat is your best bet."

As much as Sage wanted to actually get in the water and be up close and personal with the wildlife, they all agreed to go with the boat.

"Okay, then," Javier said. "Gayle, can you take us to the glass-bottomed boat port?"

Cole had just finished stowing away all the parasail equipment, so Gayle revved up the engine. "You're not going to let Russell drive?" Dev asked. Sage could tell he was joking, but Gayle looked as if she were considering it.

"No, don't!" Sage said without thinking.

Russell turned toward her, his eyes mischievous. "I saw you up there," Russell said, pointing with his finger. "I didn't need binoculars to know you were scared."

Sage felt the skin between her eyes double up as her eyes narrowed.

"You thought I was going to drop you." Russell laughed. "No way. Not with my man Dev up there with you." He grabbed Sage's shoulder and laughed some more. Dev joined in. All Sage could do was force a smile. Maybe Russell and Dev thought this race was a joke, but she didn't. And she wasn't going to let them slow the team down.

"Russell did a great job," Javier said. His tone was always understanding and kind. "But I think you would agree that we are in a hurry."

"Yes," everyone answered together.

Sage sat down next to Mari. Being teamed with strangers was definitely awkward. Sage had known the kids on her track and swim teams for years, so they knew each other's strengths and weaknesses. But they never had to work together and devise strategies. Even in relays, they each ran their leg of the race on their own. *The Wild Life* did not work that way at all.

Still, Sage had never planned to apply for *The Wild Life* by herself. She had always thought that she'd be teamed up with her sister, Caroline. Had she made the right decision? Maybe she should have waited until Caroline was ready to race. Caroline was the one person who got Sage. That would be nice right now.

Sage put the thought out of her mind. Team Red was currently in the lead. If they managed to win the race, they'd split a million dollars. That kind of money made a lot of things possible. Sage was counting on that. She needed it.

* * *

It wasn't long before the boat pulled up to a tiny port where several vessels were docked. They were all long and slender, with canopies covering the open seating area, and a cabin in the front.

One look inside explained the name "glass-bottomed." Along the center of each boat was a row of windows that stretched almost the full length of the floor and offered a clear view of the sparkling water below.

"Let's go, team!" Sage said. When she excitedly grabbed Mari's hand, the other girl's palm felt cold and clammy.

As they clambered onto the nearest boat, Javier spoke up. "It looks like another team is coming. You could wait and work with them on the next clue." He held the rope that had tied the boat to the dock in both hands.

Sage glanced up and immediately saw a huddle of purple wet suits on an approaching boat. Something told her that Team Purple was already deep in discussion about the clue. They had probably already come up with a full list of possible answers, and they probably knew which would be easiest to locate in this part of the reef.

"Smarties," Sage grumbled.

SMALLEST TO LARGEST

Plankton is a term for some of the smallest living things in the sea. The word *plankton* can refer to a plant (phytoplankton) or an animal (zooplankton), but it has to be tiny!

Plankton is a food source for all kinds of sea animals, including coral. Even some of the largest animals in the ocean eat them. The great baleen whales, from blue whales to humpbacks, filter plankton from the water.

Schools of tiny fish dine on plankton, and

larger fish then dine on the tiny fish. All marine life is connected. The largest predators rely on the tiniest plants and animals for survival.

CHAPTER 5

A SMART DECISION?

It was the first time in the race that they had the option to work with another team. Sage looked over her shoulder at Team Purple again. They were close enough now that she could see their faces: all smiling, but not one showing her teeth.

"We want to go ahead," Sage declared. "On our own."

Javier raised his eyebrows when Sage answered and then looked to her teammates. When no one said anything more, Javier tossed the crusty rope into the stern of the new boat. He stepped past Dev and Russell to talk with the boat's captain.

At once, the red team leaned forward, mesmerized by the view below. It almost seemed like they could step through the glass panes and drop into the brilliant blue water with the flowing sea grass and darting fish.

"The captain has asked if you want to go to a specific part of the reef," Javier said.

All eyes fell on Mari. "Don't look at me," she insisted, wiping sweat from her forehead.

Sage frowned. Mari had been quiet lately, even for her.

"What about that map?" Sage asked Russell.

"It tells us where we can and can't go, in order to protect the reef," he said. "But it doesn't say where we'll find an anemone and a clownfish." Everyone on Team Red knew about the classic example of symbiosis.

"Nowhere specific!" Sage yelled to the front of the boat. "Just find us some symbiosis!"

"Got it," Javier replied. "Except you have to find that yourself."

"The clownfish is the only fish that can survive the anemone's toxic sting," Dev said. "It's covered with snot so slimy that the anemone's creepy tentacles can't touch it."

"I don't think that's how it works," Sage said.

"Dev is kind of right," Mari said, her tone almost apologetic. "The clownfish has a protective layer of mucus. Scientists think it's actually a combination of both clownfish *and* anemone mucus so the anemone knows not to sting the clownfish."

"Oh, that's sweet. And disgusting," Russell commented.

"So we're looking for a zebra-striped fish in a mess of tentacles," Sage said. "This should be easy."

And it was. It took Team Red only five minutes. "Over here!" Russell called to Dev. He pointed to a vivid orange-and-white fish swimming in what looked like clump of long purple grass.

In one smooth motion, Dev lifted the ancam and aimed. *Click, click, click.* "Looks good," he assessed.

"Then send it," Sage prompted.

As they watched, a flat lemon-yellow fish with a snout like a trumpet approached the anemone. At once, a clownfish spurted forward and drove the larger fish away.

"In return for getting a safe home in the anemone's tentacles, the clownfish chases away predators," Russell said. "It's defending its turf."

"And we have to defend ours," said Sage. "We can't give up our lead."

The team quickly moved on to searching for another pair. They saw a clam as big as a cow, but no symbiosis.

Sage felt an odd ripple in her belly.

"What is that?" Russell asked, pointing over the side of the boat.

"Whatever it is, it's big." Dev held his ancam in front of his chest, frozen.

The boat began to rock with the waves. Sage caught a glimpse of a huge shadow dropping under the boat. The bottom windows filled with the murky, moving mass. Russell grabbed the railing and whipped around. "It's everywhere!"

"What's happening?" Mari asked.

The shadow seemed to be constantly shifting, curling its way around the boat. It was on all sides at once. Sage looked out over the railing again. Now she could see more clearly. The shadow was not from one giant fish, but hundreds of fish. With sleek bullet-shaped bodies, they turned with precision and speed. "It's a whole school," Sage said, gulping down air with relief. "They might be barracudas," Sage guessed after spying the silvery scales. "Mari, what do you think?"

When she glanced at her teammate, Mari was a special shade of green. She cowered in the corner, her hands pressed against her ears.

"Mari, are you okay?" Sage rushed over to the other girl's side. "Javier, Mari's sick!"

Mari flinched when Sage yelled, squinting her eyes into a web of wrinkles. She pulled away. "I feel like my brain is drowning."

"She's seasick," Javier said. "Sage, press your thumb to her wrist like this. It's a pressure point." Sage had heard about how pressure on certain parts of the body could relieve motion sickness. As soon as her thumb was in place, Javier pulled out his ancam and starting punching buttons. He studied the readout on the screen, slammed down the ancam, and rummaged in his backpack. "Mari, you've got to take this." He held out a small powdery-looking pill.

He turned to Sage. "Now the other wrist."

When Sage took Mari's sweaty hand, a familiar feeling swept over her. "You guys should keep looking," she said to Dev and Russell. "The sun is starting to set."

"I don't want to alarm you guys," announced Javier as he adjusted the contents of his backpack, "but there is a cutoff time tonight. You'll get a message on the ancam when you have to stop."

"What? How does that work?" Dev questioned, looking at his trusty device with disbelief.

"You'll just pick up with the clues in the morning, right where you left off. They can't have you searching all night."

When Javier went back to the cabin, the boys returned to their posts. Sage was torn. She didn't want the red team to lose their lead. They had to win this race. But she couldn't stand to leave Mari's side even though the younger girl had dozed off. She looked so fragile, so much like Sage's sister, Caroline.

"This has to be something." When Dev motioned, Sage joined the others. "Check out that huge moray eel resting below us, near the reef floor," he said. Sage grimaced as she took in the ghoulish frown and lifeless eyes of the eel. "Now look at its tail."

Sage's eyes followed the eel's long, tubelike body until she saw a tiny fish with a bold black stripe. "What's that other fish doing there?" Russell asked as they watched the fish nibble at the eel's burnt-orange skin. "The eel could eat him like an after-school snack."

"I think the eel likes it. I think the little fish is helping," Dev explained.

"It's probably a cleaner wrasse," Mari said from out of nowhere. When her teammates turned to look, she didn't even appear to be awake. "They eat dead skin and loose scales off of other fish."

"No way," Russell said.

"And parasites. They also eat parasites," Mari added. "They are very helpful."

"And kind of gross," Russell said.

"They are also a great example of mutualism," Sage pointed out. "The eel gets a cleaning. The wrasse gets its dinner. So shoot away." She nudged Dev, then went back to Mari, who was now the shade of a lima bean—a big improvement from spinach. After Sage sat down, she looked back at the boys. "Good work. Only one picture to go."

Russell had his back to her, and he spoke without turning around. "You know, Sage," he said, "you can't really help Mari, but you can help us."

Sage felt something tighten in her gut. Who did Russell think he was? She didn't like to be told what to do. And how did he know if she was or wasn't helping Mari? But she went back to the center of the boat and tried to remember what she had read about the reef.

Now that it was twilight, the ocean's colors seemed even deeper, like in a stained glass window.

"All the fish are darting off and hiding," Dev said.

Nighttime was bringing changes to the reef. Already, a reef shark had floated under the boat, smooth and sleek. It sped forward with just a swish of its strong tail. Soon, the sharks and other predators would take over.

A cry carried over the sloshing of water. Sage listened more closely.

"Cheering," Russell mumbled.

Sage knew what that meant. Another team had finished the clue.

Sage racked her brain. They needed only one more picture. But the sun was sinking, turning the sky into the richest shades of gold, pink, and indigo. It was only a matter of time before the race would end for the day, and Sage was certain that her team had already lost the lead.

CREATURE FEATURE

BLACKTIP REEF SHARK

SCIENTIFIC NAME: *Carcharhinus melanopterus*

TYPE: fish

RANGE: Indian and Pacific Oceans, Hawaiian Islands, Mediterranean Sea

FOOD: fish, rays, and sometimes crab, squid, and other reef creatures

Like its name suggests, the blacktip reef shark has black tips on each of its fins. It often lives in shallow water, near coral reefs. It is sleek and agile, and sometimes hunts in groups. An athletic predator, the blacktip reef shark will leap out of the water to snag a fish from the air. Even though this shark lives in waters where people often swim and scuba dive, like most shark species, it is not a big threat when people take caution.

CHAPTER 6

GOOD REFLEXES, BAD BALANCE

The Red Team couldn't make out a thing in the inky water. "It's too dark," Dev said.

Just then, the boat's underwater lights came on, and they could see that the reef was alive in a whole new way. "We can do this!" Sage cheered them on.

"Check out the coral," Dev announced. "The polyps are coming out to feed."

What looked like one piece of coral was

actually a whole colony—thousands of tiny polyps clustered together.

The coral, which had appeared lifeless just moments before, had now bloomed. Thousands of tentacles reached out to catch their dinner. Some clusters of coral looked like flowers, some like the bottom of a mushroom, others like the antlers of a deer. The polyps were all colorful and tiny.

"Come on," Sage said. "We're under the gun."

"Gun," Dev murmured.

Sage glanced at his face. His eyebrows were knotted together in thought.

"A gun makes me think of a pistol, and that makes me think of a pistol shrimp. That's it!" he exclaimed. "We should look for a goby fish and a pistol shrimp." Dev went on to tell them about the odd couple of the coral reef. "The shrimp is almost blind and builds a burrow in the sand. The goby fish shares the burrow and acts like a guard to their home."

"Sounds good," Russell said. "But are they still going to be out now that it's dark?"

"I don't know," Dev admitted.

"Well, let's look," Sage said. They all gazed into the water. Sage instinctively went to twist her earring. "Wait," she mumbled to herself, fumbling at her ear. "I lost my earring." She could feel the boys' eyes on her as she got down on her knees and searched in the creases of the rubber mats on the floor. "It's a ladybug. It must have just fallen out." When she didn't find it, she headed back to the bench where Mari was resting.

Dev looked at Russell. "I thought we were looking for symbiosis," he said, "not matching accessories."

Sage glanced back in time to see Russell swallow a smirk. They were always joking. They wouldn't understand.

She didn't see the earring on the seat. Again, she reached for her bare ear. This time, her fingers caught on something. The earring had been snagged in her hair, and her fingers had knocked it loose.

Out of the corner of her eye, Sage saw it slip off her shoulder toward the dark water. She threw herself after it. The ladybug hit her palm and her

fingers closed around it at once. Good thing she had quick reflexes! Too bad she had bad balance. Half her body was tipped over the boat's railing. In seconds, she hit the sea headfirst with a splash.

She was fine. Wet, but fine.

Dev's and Russell's faces appeared over the side of the boat. When they saw her, they exploded with laughter.

"That was graceful," Russell said.

"Practically slow motion," Dev added.

Sage scowled. Why was everything funny to them?

"Too bad it's so dark. I would have loved to have seen your face," said Russell. Sage couldn't believe he was smiling. "Here," Russell offered, holding out his hand. "I'll pull you up."

Sage rolled her eyes. "I can swim to the ladder, thanks. You guys should be looking for symbiosis. Remember? Time's running out."

"Oh, is that what you were doing?" Dev slapped Russell a high five, and the two boys disappeared toward the center of the boat.

Sage was furious with herself. Not only had she cost them valuable time, she had given the boys something else to laugh about, as if they needed her help with that.

The good news was that her hand was still clenched in a fist. She might have made a fool of herself, but she had her earring.

As soon as she was back in the boat, she zipped the earring into her backpack. Then she positioned herself next to the boys, as determined as ever.

"What's that?" Russell asked. Sage heard it, too. A low buzzing was growing louder. Dev pulled out the ancam. It was flashing red.

"Time's up for the day," Javier announced as he entered the main cabin. He sat down next to Mari. "Race is back on at eight o'clock tomorrow morning. You can't submit any photos until then."

"We know," Sage said, looking down. "We know."

When the glass-bottomed boat pulled up to a jetty, the kids all bid the captain farewell. "There's a resort on the other side of the island, but we're good to hang out here for a while," Javier said, grabbing a cooler. "It'll be good for Mari to have some time on solid ground. The yacht will come and pick us up later."

Sage helped Mari to the beach. As soon as the

younger girl sat down, Sage took off her water sandals and started pacing in the fine sand. Even as the others took their places on the blanket to eat, Sage didn't join them. She grabbed some grapes and walked close to the tree line. With everything that had happened, she had too much nervous energy to sit down.

It was only moments into their picnic dinner when Mari let out a yelp.

"What's wrong?" Sage asked.

"It's not me," Mari insisted. "It's that sea turtle."

Near the edge of the waves, a lone sea turtle pushed its way up the sand. In an instant, Mari was by the turtle's side. "She's stranded. Sea turtles don't just come up on land, not this time of year."

"You're right," Javier said. "They close this island for part of the year so sea turtles can safely lay their eggs, but it's too early for that."

On land, the reptile could only scoot. Unaccustomed to being out of the water, its breath was shallow. Mari respected the tortoise's space, but knelt down to get a better look. As her gaze fell on a front flipper, she flinched. "She's hurt. There's a net wrapped around her flipper and her neck," she said, pointing to where the thin threads dug into the turtle's scaly skin.

Javier stood and turned to the group. "You guys, stay here. There is an animal rescue center at the resort. They'll know how to help." With only a glance backward, Javier took off for the other side of the island.

Russell knelt down close to Mari. "How do you know it's a girl?" he wondered.

Mari looked at him and smirked. "I don't," she confessed. "I just guessed."

Dev snorted. "Mari doesn't know *everything*."

Mari tilted her head to one side. "Well, I guessed based on the fact that her tail isn't very long. The tails of male green turtles stick way out of their shell, so this one is probably a female."

"That's what I'm talking about," Russell said with exaggerated pride. "We missed you today, Mari."

"Sorry I was so sick." Mari dragged her finger through the sand.

"No worries. We got two good shots," Sage answered. "We'll get the last one in the morning." Sage brushed biscuit crumbs from her hands.

"Can I ask which ones we found?"

They quickly gave her a recap. Sage was surprised that Mari had missed almost everything that had happened on the boat.

"What about coral and the algae that live inside?" Mari asked, tightening her braid.

Of course! Sage could hardly believe it. Algae is a simple form of plant. The coral gives the algae a safe home. The algae provides the coral with energy and oxygen, which plants create during photosynthesis. How could she have forgotten that? Her sister would have thought of it in two seconds. Caroline would love teasing Sage for not coming up with it.

"I can take that shot first thing tomorrow," Dev said, sounding both frustrated and relieved.

The four teammates fell silent.

"What are you guys going to do with the money if we win?" Russell asked, picking up a green piece of fruit that had fallen off a vine. He motioned to Dev, who stood up and readied himself for a pass.

Dev caught the prickly fruit and gave his hand a shake. "I'd give most of it to my mom so she could start her own business," Dev said. "You?" He threw the fruit back.

"I'd donate some to my town, for our rec center." Russell jumped up to make the catch. "After I got a new cell phone and Xbox, of course."

"I'd buy some clothes that weren't hand-me-downs. Then I'd give some to organizations that help wildlife," Mari offered.

When Mari said that, Sage thought of her sister again. It's exactly what Caroline would do. Caroline was always thinking of the big picture, and she was sick of hand-me-downs, too.

Sage could hear people approaching through the wooded path. She turned back to her teammates. "I just want to win," she said, standing up.

"Yeah, we got that," Russell said under his breath.

"But you want to find your earring more," Dev added. Sage thought they were joking, but she couldn't be sure.

Sage was grateful for the night's shadows. If

they expected her to say something, to take their bait, they would be disappointed.

Javier came back with two people from the resort. The workers had seen many stranded sea turtles in their years on the island. Some had been caught in nets; some had been hit by boat propellers or attacked by sharks; others had eaten trash and become sick. Sylvie, one of the rescue workers, had a good feeling that they'd be able to help the turtle that Mari had found.

"We'll take good care of her," Sylvie promised.

Mari had a hard time leaving the sea turtle but she was still tired from being sick, so she didn't put up much of a fight. Javier herded everyone toward the yacht. No one said a word as they walked along the jetty. When they reached the lower deck, Javier pushed another chalky pill into Mari's hand. "There's a storm coming. It shouldn't be bad, but be prepared," he said.

Everyone nodded and went to their cabins with only murmurs of "good night." Sage wanted to say something positive, to get the team pumped for the race tomorrow, but she couldn't find the words. She doubted whether they would even listen to her. She wasn't pulling her weight. She had let herself get distracted from their goal. That wasn't what good leaders do.

Mari gave Sage a faint smile as she swallowed her pill and climbed to the top bunk. If they had completed the clue, they could have stayed up and talked about the next challenge. Sage thought that they should try to plan their strategy for the morning, but no one seemed up for it. She convinced herself that everyone was too tired, but she could hear Dev and Russell whispering in their cabin long after the lights went out.

CREATURE FEATURE

GREEN TURTLE

SCIENTIFIC NAME: *Chelonia mydas*

TYPE: reptile

RANGE: tropical waters all over the world

FOOD: as adults: only algae, grasses, and

other plants; when young: plants and some

small animals such as worms, crabs, and snails

You might have trouble identifying a green turtle by its shell. It's not typically green. Neither is its skin. This species gets its name for the colorful fat *under* its skin. A green turtle's shell, or carapace, is sometimes green and usually mixed with brown, gray, or black.

Amazingly, green turtles can live over 100 years, and can weigh up to 450 pounds. But they are endangered. They have countless predators, and many die as eggs or in their first few years.

Even though they hatch on the beach, green turtles spend almost their entire lives in the water. Males never leave the ocean. Females leave only to lay their eggs on the beach where they were born, just like their mothers did before them, even if it means swimming hundreds of miles to get there.

CHAPTER 7

A BAD MORNING

The waves that rocked the yacht all night were still sloshing in Sage's head when she woke. For once, she decided to go back to sleep. She always woke up too early anyway. She pulled the sheet over her head until she heard a knock on the cabin door.

"Sage?" Mari said. "It's seven fifty-five. Dev is about to take the picture of the coral and algae. Maybe you want to get up so you're ready?"

"What?" Sage screeched. "Why didn't my alarm go off?" She was out of bed, pulling on her swimsuit, latching her watch, and tying back her hair in a smooth sequence of moves choreographed for efficiency.

"I thought you might need the sleep," Mari explained.

"That's not for you to decide," Sage said. "I need to be up." She had a race to run and she couldn't do it from bed. What had happened to her alarm?

She rushed up the stairs to find Dev leaning far over the side of the boat. *Click, click, click.* "Got it!" he said. "That example of symbiosis was pretty easy to find. Too bad we didn't get it yesterday."

Sage looked at her watch. "It's only seven fifty-nine. You better wait until eight to send it in."

"And good morning to you, too!" Dev said, all bright and shiny.

Sage rolled her eyes and grabbed a banana. "Didn't the storm bug any of you?"

"Not really," admitted Russell.

Sage fumbled with the rubbery banana peel. What else was going to go wrong today?

"Looks like it's wet suit time again," Dev announced, still abnormally cheery. "Here's our clue."

```
    Creeping on the ocean floor
With eight or twenty arms or more,
   It's an unexpected thorny beast
   That gobbles coral for a feast.
```

"Thorny, lots of arms, gobbles coral," Mari repeated. "That's the crown-of-thorns starfish."

"All right," Dev said. "Good to have you back, Mari!"

Sage nodded in agreement as she took a bite of her banana. At least Mari was back to normal.

"I looked at the map," Russell explained. "Our boat's actually already docked in a good spot, so we could just dive in."

The teammates looked at one another. Sage hurried to swallow.

"Then let's go," Dev said, and everyone grabbed their snorkel masks.

As they pulled on their flippers, Mari reminded them what they were looking for. The correct starfish species had many arms with lots of venomous spines on each one. It looked a little like a toxic cactus. It could be bright purple, orange, or red. "Most importantly," Mari said, "it will be on the coral. Devouring it."

The rest of the team was ready.

"Hurry up, Sage," Dev said. "Why are we always waiting on you?"

"What?" Sage scowled, tugging on her flippers.

"It's just a joke. You know, because usually you're always ready before us, urging us on," Dev said, and then jumped into the water.

Sage sighed. It really was not her morning.

At last, she was in the water and on the move. Life burst from every nook and cranny of the reef, a bouquet of color. The sea wasn't too deep here. The plants—including the algae in the coral— needed the sun.

There was so much to see, Sage had to remind herself that they were searching for one thing:

the crown-of-thorns starfish. They had to find it soon if they were going to win. The four teammates stayed close, and Sage willingly took the lead. Her eyes were bombarded with color: electric-blue fish, lime-green sea grass, orange bursts of coral.

Sage was so at home in the water, it took her a few moments to realize she had gone ahead on her own. When she looked around, Dev, Mari, and Russell were all crowded together, looking at something. As soon as she swam back to join them, Sage saw what they were staring at: the blinding whiteness of an entire island of reef robbed of its color.

Then she saw the crown-of-thorns. It was larger than any starfish she had ever seen, with more arms radiating from its center—each one covered

with prickly spines for protection. But it was the coral that needed protecting. Sage knew that the starfish's mouth was on its underside. Right now, that mouth was eating the polyps right off of their white limestone skeleton. Only a few branches of the staghorn coral remained the original bright apple green. When Sage moved to look away, she realized that there was another—no, two, no, three—crown-of-thorns starfish on coral nearby.

Dev zoomed in on the starfish and snapped the shot, then they all kicked to the surface.

"You sent it in?" Sage confirmed. Dev nodded, and they waited, treading water.

Sage turned to Mari. "You okay?" she asked.

Mari gave a small smile. "This starfish is actually pretty cool," she said between raspy breaths. "It can spit out its stomach, more or less. Then its stomach digests the polyps right there, on the coral. When it's broken them all down, the starfish pulls its stomach back inside and moves on."

"Mari, your idea of cool is kind of bizarre," Russell said. His nose and upper lip were all crinkled up.

Sage agreed. It sounded disgusting. In her opinion, the crown-of-thorns starfish was a more vicious predator than any shark.

"That was quick," Dev announced, focusing on the ancam screen. "We have our next clue."

Sage hoped that whatever it was, they could solve it quickly and get to the finish line in first place.

OUTBREAK

In a healthy ecosystem, predators like the crown-of-thorns starfish play an important role. These starfish help keep balance in the reef. They do this by eating the fastest growing corals, like the staghorn. But when the number of crown-of-thorns starfish skyrockets, they eat too much coral and jeopardize the health of the reef.

The life cycle of the crown-of-thorns starfish may help explain how an outbreak happens.

Only adult crown-of-thorns starfish feed on coral. The larvae—a very early form—eat plankton. Young starfish eat algae, a plant. When there is more food for the starfish at these younger stages, there will eventually be more adult starfish eating the coral. And since adult crown-of-thorns starfish are venomous, they have few natural predators.

Recently, warm ocean water and other conditions have allowed more young starfish to thrive. There are now so many adults that they are destroying large parts of the reef, and the coral cannot grow back fast enough.

CHAPTER 8
NOT A MERMAID

Related to the elephant

But with a tail like a whale,

It might have inspired tales

of mermaids,

But has longer whiskers than locks.

"Finally!" Dev cried. "A clue that doesn't rhyme!"

"Finally!" Russell cried. "A clue that I know the

answer to. It's the dugong. Because the clue's

about locks of hair, not combination locks. Those things drive me crazy."

Sage quickly thought ahead. They had already been in the water awhile. "Is everyone good to go?"

"Sure. We should just search here, right," Dev said. "Maybe we could save time and catch up."

Sage looked at Mari again. The younger girl wasn't a strong swimmer to begin with, and she had been so sick the day before. Sage knew she should insist that they stop to rest, but she also yearned to keep going, to strive for the win.

"Let's do it," Mari said to Sage's surprise.

They all dunked their faces in the water and started to search.

Sage wanted to find a dugong as fast as

possible. The faster Sage worked, the sooner they would all get a break.

Sage remembered that sometimes, to escape sharks, dugongs would swim to the deeper waters of the reef. So she separated from the others and followed a winding path through the underwater towers of coral. The ocean floor began to drop away. The early morning sun did not reach to the bottom of the ocean floor here, and the water seemed murkier, the shadows darker.

Sage sensed something move below her. She squinted, trying to focus. There it was again. She couldn't get a good look. If she wanted to find out what it was, she'd have to go deeper and dive with the snorkel on. She took a full breath and plunged down, pushing against the water.

Whatever it was, it slid under a shelf of coral. In the darkness, Sage couldn't tell how big it was. She knew dugongs were shy. Maybe this mystery creature was the answer to the clue. Sage was starting to run out of air, but she worked her way lower.

She was now even with the reef floor. All at once, a bundle of tiny arms burst from under the coral. The creature scuttled toward her with jagged movements. Its body was the size of a baseball. The wriggling bundle was covered in tiny rings that began to glow an intense peacock blue.

Something strong seized Sage from behind and dragged her to the surface. She tried to scream, but water surged into her mouth. The

sun flashed in her eyes, and her body quaked with coughs. Her arms lashed out as she tried to fight off whatever had grabbed her.

"It's me!"

It took Sage a moment to register the voice. Then Mari appeared in front of her. "Blue-ringed octopus!" the younger girl sputtered. "More deadly than jellyfish." She had Sage's arm now and was pulling her away.

"No," Sage yelled, finally finding her voice. She ripped her wrist from Mari's grasp. "What are you doing? What are you doing here?" Mari turned back, confused.

Sage's mask was foggy. She could barely even see Mari, and she didn't want the other girl to see her. "You don't look out for me. That's not your job. I can take care of myself."

"We got it!" a voice called out. It sounded far away. "Sage! Mari!"

Sage was still trying to catch her breath. Water dripped from her forehead down the tip of her nose. Instinctively her hand rushed to her ear. She still had her earring.

"Russell got a photo of the dugong!" Dev's voice called again.

"We're here," Mari answered. She waved as the two snorkel pipes came into view.

The boys' faces were stretched with smiles. "It was awesome! He got it in like record time," Dev said. "We're still waiting for the next clue to come in, but show them," he prompted Russell.

Just as Russell reached out to display the ancam screen, a shadow passed below. "No way. There it is again," he said, pointing underwater.

The four kids lowered their faces into the water.

Sage forced herself to take calm, even breaths through the snorkel. She tried to forget what had just happened and focus on the dugong.

It was funny to think that the dugong, with its short, wide trunk, could have inspired stories of mermaids. But it was graceful, floating along the reef floor. Sage had always felt so at home in the water. Now she just wanted to be anywhere else.

After the dugong had passed, the red team lifted their heads. "Let's go back to the boat," Mari said. "Sage found a blue-ringed octopus, or it found her. They aren't common this far north, but I don't want to stick around and see it again."

"Whoa, those things are nasty," Dev said.

The boys looked at Sage. She didn't say anything. The octopus hadn't stung her, but she still felt stunned.

By the time they were back on the boat, they had received their next clue. It was a set of coordinates. "It must be where we get the next challenge," Russell said.

"I'll show it to Javier and the captain," Dev suggested, looking to Sage for approval.

Sage nodded, then went down to the girls' cabin and sat on the edge of her bed. She found her family photo in her bag. Since no phones or cameras were allowed, this was all she had. She stared at it for a while.

When she heard the yacht's motor rev up, she convinced herself to get her head back in the game.

She found the rest of the team on the deck. They stopped talking at the sight of her. She had expected that. It had happened a lot over the last year. In this case, it was a good thing. It gave them a chance to get their heads back in the race, too.

But then Russell pushed Mari forward.

"Sage," her teammate said, "we're worried."

Sage took a breath and felt her shoulders draw back. Her chin lifted.

"I went after you on purpose. We need to stick together. That's what teams do."

It took Sage a moment to realize Mari was talking about what had happened at the reef.

Mari looked at the ground. Her cheek twitched. "I don't care what you say. It is my job to look after you. It's all our jobs. We have to look after each other."

Sage looked out to sea, avoiding her teammates' faces.

"Listen," Russell said. "We know you want to be the team leader. You're good at it. And Mari's smart about animals, and Dev's good with gadgets, and I'm whatever I am. But we're all more than that. And you don't have to laugh at our jokes or tell us what you want to do with the prize money. But we are a team. And you can't tell us not to have your back."

Sage shifted her eyes to look in the other direction, but they locked with Russell's. He held her gaze and didn't look away.

"Look," she began, her voice soft. "I was supposed to apply for *The Wild Life* with my sister, but then she was in an accident." Sage hadn't told the story for so long. It had been almost a year—

a year of doctors' appointments and physical therapy. It seemed like forever. "The doctors said she couldn't race, and I refused to do it without her. But my parents thought it would be good for me." She paused and let her eyes sweep over her teammates' faces. "They probably just wanted me out of the house. So I gave in, and promised myself that I would win. I would win so I could take Caroline everywhere she's always wanted to go."

Sage didn't tell them about how she felt responsible for what had happened to her sister. It had been her job to look after Caroline at the track meet, but she hadn't even seen when Caroline had broken her shoulder and her arm. Sage had been competing on the other side of the track. Caroline wouldn't have even been there if it hadn't been for Sage.

Sage also didn't tell them that her earrings were a good luck gift from Caroline, just for the race. But the way Russell, Dev, and Mari looked at her, Sage knew she didn't have to tell them any of these things.

"Sometimes, during the race, I get caught up in all of that. I want to win so much, I try to take charge of everything. It feels like the only thing I can do," she said. "And then, when Mari got sick, it reminded me of Caroline. Then all I wanted was to make sure she would be okay."

Sage was grateful for the silence that followed.

"And I was fine," Mari said after a while. "You looked out for me, and I wanted to do the same for you."

Sage couldn't look at Mari, but she gave a slight nod. Sage wasn't used to anyone looking out for her. That had always been her job.

"I get it," Russell added, his arms crossed. "It's a good reason to want to win."

"Yeah, I'm all for winning," Dev admitted, "but your sister would want you to have fun. You need to stop thinking about her accident. She'd want you to get the most out of it. She wouldn't want you to run this race just to get first place."

"Yeah," Russell added. "She'd want you to have good times, and answer clues that end in rhymes." Russell burst out laughing at his attempt at poetry. Dev rolled his eyes, horrified.

"You started it, man," Russell claimed. "You said, 'Run this race, just to get first place.' Next year you should get a job writing the clues."

The look on Dev's face was hilarious, and Sage was soon doubled over with laughter, wiping fresh tears from her eyes. It was not long before Mari gave in. The red team had lost it. They were in no condition to run a race.

CREATURE FEATURE

DUGONG

SCIENTIFIC NAME: *Dugong dugon*

TYPE: mammal

RANGE: coastal waters of the Indian Ocean, Pacific Ocean, and neighboring seas

FOOD: sea grass

While it has a tail with two flukes, similar to a whale, the dugong is more closely related to an elephant. But other than the color of its thick skin, the dugong has few physical traits in common with its big-eared cousins. Dugongs don't even have earflaps! They do, however, have a large snout with a long upper lip for picking sea grass, which is this picky herbivore's first choice for breakfast, lunch, and dinner. Its love of grass is the reason for its nickname: sea cow. This name can also refer to the dugong's close relative, the manatee.

CHAPTER 9

WHALE OF A FINISH

Javier seemed taken aback when he found the team in a huddle of giggles. "I'm glad you're having a good time, but we're almost to the coordinates," he announced.

"Thank you," Russell said. "We are having a good time." Then he added, "I hope that's not a crime."

Dev whacked him in the stomach with the back of his arm. "Sage, can you please tell us what to do so he'll stop?"

Sage wasn't sure what to say. Was this her job? Was this what she needed to do for the team? She looked to Mari, but the other girl just shook her head.

Sage sniffed back the laughter and pushed herself off of the deck floor. "Someone get binoculars," she said, surveying where the boat was headed. "We need to figure out what the next challenge will be."

Dev scrambled to his feet, grabbed his binoculars, and focused them into the distance.

Javier turned toward the main cabin. The guide seemed relieved that Team Red was back on track.

Dev assessed that there was a small fleet of kayaks docked at a floating platform. Farther in the distance was an island. "There's a pennant

with the Wild Life logo on it!" Dev exclaimed. "It's on the beach."

"You think we just need to get from the platform to the island and we'll be done?" Mari asked.

"Well, we could ask Team Purple," Dev said. "I can see someone in a purple shirt already on the beach."

Sage shook her head. Team Purple was impressive.

As the yacht's engine decreased to a purr, Sage's heart rate nearly doubled. The boat pulled up, and the team climbed right from the boat's ladder to the floating dock. When they looked back to Javier, he had something in his hand. It was a large red key. He handed it to Sage.

"Thanks," she said, and they all waved to their trusty chaperone.

"It must be for the kayaks," Dev said, motioning to the two-person boats tied to the dock. He quickly examined the key and the various locks. "Our key will only work on the red one."

Sage calculated that there was one canoe missing: the purple one.

How much of a lead did the Smarties have? When Sage looked to the Wild Life flag, she could see that there was a kayak in the water. It wasn't even halfway to the beach.

"Look! They're not that far ahead!" Sage

exclaimed. It wasn't the same, racing for second place, but Team Red still had something to prove. "Mari, you're in front. Russell in the back." Sage held the shell steady as her teammates slid into place, and Dev handed them paddles. "Russell, you up to coming back for us?"

"Yeah," he said, already pushing off.

"Hurry!" she yelled.

As she watched them paddle toward the island, she wondered how long it would take Russell to row back.

"You know, it's a good thing you're so good at taking charge," Dev said. "Otherwise, you would be pretty annoying."

Sage glanced at Dev, who smiled.

"Thanks," she said. "I guess." She reached for her ladybug earring.

They both watched as Russell and Mari paddled through the water.

"They're gaining on the purple team," Dev pointed out.

"They are," Sage agreed. She could tell that Eliza was in the purple kayak with one of her teammates. Sage guessed Eliza had rowed the other two purple team members to the beach. She must be worn out by now.

"It feels weird," Dev said, "just watching them."

Sage looked toward the pennant, flapping in the breeze on the island.

"I don't suppose you want to swim?" she asked, her arms and legs already pulsing with energy.

"Is that a joke?" Dev asked.

"You might have noticed I'm not good at jokes," she answered.

"Then let's do it," Dev said. "I kind of did the math. I bet we can swim it faster than Russell can kayak back and forth two more times."

"I bet you're right," Sage said. She moved to the edge of the dock and bent her knees. Dev did the same. "Ready, set, go!" Together, they dove in.

This felt good and right. She was on the move, not so much racing as making progress, side by side with a teammate.

They'd swum several strokes when Sage thought she heard a scream. She immediately pulled up and treaded water, trying to figure it out. She heard the high-pitched sound again, but this time it was more of a delighted squeal. Dev had stopped, too, and they both looked ahead to where Russell and Mari were paddling. Sage

focused just in time to see a mighty set of fringed flukes splash the water, only yards from the red kayak.

"That whale isn't giving them enough clear-ance," Dev said. "Bull Gordon could take points away for that."

Sage smiled. At this point, she didn't care about clearance or clues or ancams. She did care that Mari had been able to see a whale, perhaps closer than she had even wanted.

She also noticed that the purple kayak had not stopped. It had continued to the beach at a steady rate, plodding toward first place.

Mari pumped both arms, holding her paddle in the air. Sage felt a surge of energy, too, and pushed her way through the water with strong, steady strokes. She felt the burn in her muscles.

She found a good rhythm, and Dev stayed by her side.

Soon they were stumbling up the sandy beach together.

"What were you guys thinking?" Russell asked, reaching out to help Dev.

"We just wanted to get here, to finish," said Dev.

Mari grabbed Sage's arm as they walked up the beach.

Sage glanced at her friend. "That humpback," she gasped.

"I know." Mari's eyes sparkled. "I know."

They half staggered, half ran up the path toward the Wild Life pennant. There, they saw Bull Gordon with his thumbs thrust through his belt loops again. Even on the beach, he sported his felt fedora.

They came to a stop before him, all in a line.

"Team Red," he announced. "You are in second place. Congratulations."

"Thank you," Sage answered, her voice in chorus with her teammates.

"You lost your lead," Bull said. "But you seem okay with that."

A hundred responses ran through Sage's head. A hundred excuses. But they didn't matter. "Yeah," she said. "I think we are. At least, I am." She looked to her teammates, not wanting to speak for them.

"We got through a lot on this leg," Russell said.

"And we got to see a lot," Mari added. This comment made Sage smile. Mari was a lot like Caroline. She was also very much herself. So were Dev and Russell. They all had their strengths, but their characters went well beyond that.

"Yeah, what they said," Dev answered, motioning toward Mari, Russell, and Sage. Then they all looked back to Bull Gordon.

"Okay, then," Bull responded. "You'll be the second team to start the next course. Hope you know a lot about Arctic animals and their ecosystem. You'll need all the help you can get there."

Sage felt her heart skip at the thought of another leg of the race. It was another chance for Team Red to prove itself. As they walked over to the concession table to join the purple team, Sage thought again about what Bull Gordon had said. She was excited about the Arctic and what they could encounter there: polar bears, glaciers, gray wolves. But where *The Wild Life* went next wasn't all that important, because Sage knew something Bull Gordon didn't. No matter where they ended up, she already had all the help she needed. Her friends had already taught her a lot about being a team. Maybe, one day, they'd even teach her how to take a joke.

Want to know what happens when *The Wild Life*

heads to the freezing Alaskan tundra? Read on

for a sneak peek at the next race course in

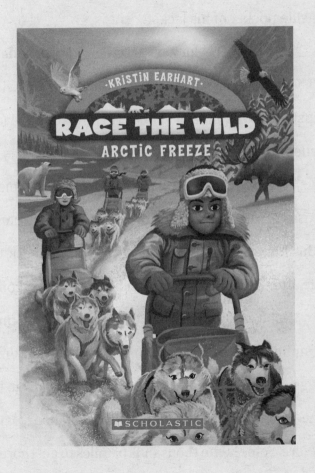

Once they sent in a picture of a grizzly, they would get the next clue. Dev patted the team's trusty ancam. He had it safely stashed in the inside pocket of his jacket.

"We may see lots of grizzlies," Mari added. "They know that the salmon are starting to swim upstream this time of year, returning to the place where they were born to spawn."

"I know what spawning means in a video game," Russell called back from the bank of the stream. "But I don't think the salmon are coming back to life after being killed by an acid-breathing dragon."

"Not exactly," Mari said without even cracking a smile. "Spawning is when fish lay and fertilize eggs, so new fish can be born. Salmon do it in the exact same place where they hatched years before. Some swim thousands of miles to get there."

Dev admired Mari. She had all this knowledge, but she was super humble about it.

"So, if Dev is right, the river will be on the other side of that hill," Sage announced. "We're climbing up to see if there are any bears." She, Russell, and Javier quickly disappeared over the grassy bank while Mari and Dev made their way to the edge of the stream.

Dev was starting to feel like his head was back in the race. He thought ahead to what angle might be good for the grizzly photo. The sun was strong. He'd have to be careful that it didn't mess up the light in the picture. Sometimes there was only enough time for one good shot.

With his mind on the photo, he didn't notice that the floor of the stream bed was getting mucky as they neared the shore. Mari must not have noticed either. The water was above his knees when he realized he was stuck.

"I can't move," Mari announced from behind him.

"I can't either," Dev said, his tone even.

"I mean it," Mari said. Her pitch was rising high above the rush of the brisk water.

"I know, but you have to stay calm," Dev said. "I think we're stuck in some kind of quicksand. If you struggle, you could sink deeper." Dev's words came out slow and steady, but his mind was in a frenzied whirl—trying to solve the problem like a puzzle, trying to do what he did best.

READ *ARCTIC FREEZE* TO FIND OUT WHAT HAPPENS NEXT!

WHEN DISASTER STRIKES, THE ONLY THING YOU CAN COUNT ON IS YOURSELF!

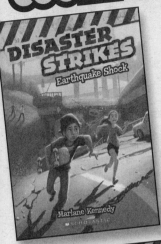

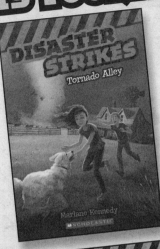

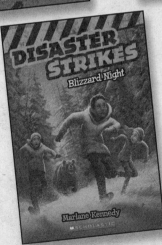

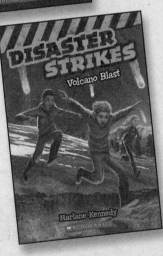

Earthquakes in California. Tornados in Oklahoma. Blizzards in Michigan. Volcanoes in Alaska. Find out what these kids do to launch into survival mode on disaster day.

The Rescue Princesses

These are no ordinary princesses—
they're Rescue Princesses!